The TARTAN TRAMPOLINE and The Red Shoes

Written by
JENNIFER BAKER

Illustrated by
SARAH CAMPBELL

The Tartan Trampoline and the Red Shoes

Text copyright © Jennifer Baker, 2021
Illustrations copyright © Sarah Campbell, 2021

ISBN 978-1-9993668-7-2 (paperback)

Second printing October 2021

Published by
Mòr Media Limited
Argyll, Scotland

www.mormedia.co.uk
Book design by Helen Crossan

For Matilda Wai Ying

Manny and Effie were brother and sister and Tilly was their cousin. All year they lived in big cities where they went to school and had lots of friends but, when the school holidays came, they got on a train which took them to the Highlands of Scotland where their grandmother lived. Her house was at the side of a loch on a tiny island.

They had to catch a ferry to get there, and Allan the ferryman always had a great welcoming shout for them when they got on.

'Hello you three—back again? Well, the island is very pleased to see you!'

The children loved Allan, and they loved their grandmother who was always waiting on the slip for them.

She was called Shayjay but no one knew why. She just was.

The children were always really excited when they arrived on the island but this time they were even more excited because they were going to fly on the Tartan Trampoline. Nobody else knew that the Tartan Trampoline could fly. It was magic that only Manny, Effie and Tilly knew about. Even Shayjay, who put the trampoline up in the summer and took it down in the winter, didn't know about the magic.

3

'Is the Tartan Trampoline up, Shayjay?' asked Tilly.

'Of course,' said Shayjay. 'All ready and waiting for you.'

When they arrived at Shayjay's house at the end of a long track, they saw the huge trampoline right away and immediately kicked off their shoes and climbed the steps. They all started bouncing high, doing somersaults and star jumps and lots of other skilful things.

But they were tired after their long journey and so went in, had their tea and went to bed in the bedroom at the top of the house. You see, they wanted the morning to come very quickly, because they knew what was going to happen. And it did.

When they woke up, they could see the dawn through the windows in the roof. What was much more important, though, was the big wind howling around the house. They looked at each other with huge smiles.

'Let's go,' whispered Tilly. They put on warm clothes and tiptoed downstairs so that they wouldn't waken Shayjay.

As soon as they were outside, they ran around the field whooping wildly but they could hardly hear each other because the wind was so loud. Then they climbed the steps to the trampoline and lay down, peering over the edge.

They were all a bit nervous as well as excited. The trampoline gave a bit of a squeak and a sigh, then the wind picked it up and swirled them through the sky. They hung on for dear life. They were so high that they could hardly see the island below.

The sky was pink with the rising sun but, as the Tartan Trampoline flew on, the weather began to change.

The clouds got darker and, when the children looked down, they could hardly see the loch below. Swathes of mist that looked like white veils moved back and forth across the grey water.

They began to shiver and were just beginning to get really cold when the wind dropped. The trampoline floated gently down into a castle courtyard. All they could see were grey walls going up and up to grey parapets and a grey sky.

'Let's go inside,' Tilly shivered. 'I'm freezing.'

They ran towards a huge wooden door. At first they thought it was locked but, when all three pushed hard, it opened with a long CREEEEEEAK which was a bit frightening, but they went in anyway—they were so cold. Inside it was only slightly warmer.

'Do you think they've turned the heating off?' said Effie.

'I think they usually have big fires in castles,' said Tilly.

They all looked at a huge empty fireplace.

'Not here,' said Manny. 'I'm glad we all put these jumpers on this morning.'

They walked across the great hall towards one of the many doors in the wall.

'Let's try this,' said Tilly. 'Maybe it'll be warmer in here.'

'Do you think we should?' said Manny. 'This isn't our place, you know.'

'Oh come *on*,' said Tilly impatiently but, just as she was about to put her hand on the door, they heard a voice behind them. It was quite a posh voice, like you hear on the television news programmes.

'May I help you?'

They turned around to see a tall, thin woman standing on the stone stairs. She was wearing a long, grey, old-fashioned frock that had silver glittery braid on it. She had a pale face and grey hair but what they noticed the *most* was that her feet were entirely bare and were *blue* with cold.

'Yes,' said Tilly. 'We've been travelling quite a long way and then the weather changed and we hoped we could get a bit warm in here before we go on. I am Tilly and these are my cousins, Manny and Effie.'

'Well, you've come to the wrong place,' said the posh woman. 'We've no heating here at all.'

'Why don't you light the fire?' asked Manny.

'No logs,' said the woman.

'Can you not cut some?' asked Effie.

The posh woman laughed coldly. 'I don't cut logs, but even if I did, I can't go out with no shoes on.'

'I'll do it!' said Tilly.

'You're not allowed to use an axe, Tilly, don't be mad. None of us are.' said Effie.

Tilly gave Effie a hard look but didn't say anything else.

Just then, another door opened, and a girl about the same age as Tilly came skipping into the room. She was dressed in grey like her mother, but her dress was short and she was wearing grey leggings. Her hair was like shiny silver and was very long, and her feet, too, were as *blue* as *blue*.

'Hello,' she said without stopping skipping.

'She's pretty good,' thought Tilly.

'Hello,' said Tilly. 'You're very good at skipping.'

'Practice,' said the girl. 'I have to do it all the time to keep warm.'

'Actually,' said Effie, 'is there nobody who can bring the logs to you?'

'It seems a bit silly to keep skipping all the time,' said Manny.

'Well, you see,' said the girl, who wasn't even out of breath, 'it's not allowed. It's all to do with the shoes, you see.'

'Shoes?' The three children looked at each other. This posh girl and her posh mother both seemed a bit mad.

'Come into the kitchen. It's a bit warmer there.'

They followed the girl through yet another door and down some stone steps to the basement.

'I'm Annabel,' said the girl. The children told her their names as they went down the stairs, Annabel still skipping.

'I wish I could skip downstairs,' thought Tilly.

When they reached the kitchen, Annabel stopped skipping. There were lots of people working there, coming and going, and very busy making salads and ice cream and other cold foods. Every one of them was dressed in grey clothes. They had pale faces and grey hair although some of the younger ones had silver hair like Annabel's. And every one of them had bare, blue feet. Annabel poured them cups of cold water and all four of them perched on stools.

'Shoes?' asked Tilly. 'Tell us about the shoes.'

'Well,' said Annabel, 'last year, for my birthday, my mother—'

'The grey woman we saw?' interrupted Manny.

'Yes. Her name's Tabitha, though I call her Mama.

17

'So ... she took me into town for my birthday, and we were looking round all the shops at toys and dresses and things—pretty boring, really,' the three children nodded, 'when suddenly I saw these red shiny shoes and I wanted to try them on but Mama said they were far too big. I really wanted to try them, so she said 'cos it was my birthday, I could. They were too big, so she said I had to take them off again, and I didn't want to, so I had a big tantrum.'

They all smiled sympathetically— they knew what having a tantrum felt like.

'So what happened?' asked Effie.

'Well, this man came up. He was a bit frightening-looking but he smiled at Mama and so she smiled back. Then he said, "I can make the shoes fit, if you like." But Mama said "No", so I had another tantrum and this time I nearly made myself sick!'

Tilly, Effie and Manny were very impressed. None of them had had as big a tantrum as that.

'Then what?'

'Well, then Mama said "Yes", and the shoes fitted! And everybody cheered, and the man visited us often after that.'

Just then, Tabitha came in.

'Yes,' she said in her posh voice, 'and that man whom we all thought was so kind was actually a wicked wizard who wanted our castle and all our money, and when we got the police to take him away, he cursed us and made a magic wind that whipped off all our shoes and threw them up into that Scots pine on the top of the mountain. He said we'd never be warm till we got the shoes back.'

She pointed out of the window and they saw the tree on top of the highest mountain.

'Well, could you not get a mountaineer or a helicopter or something?' asked Manny. 'Or buy new shoes?'

'No,' said Tabitha, 'because that's not magic and only magic can break the spell.'

'We have a magic trampoline!' shouted Tilly.

'But we can't steer it,' said Effie.

'Doesn't matter,' said Manny. 'It steered us here!'

They all ran outside and, yes, the trampoline steered itself to the top of the mountain and there, at the very top of the Scots pine, were Annabel's shiny red shoes, crossed together like a star. All the way down the tree were lots of pairs of shoes tied together by their laces and hanging like Christmas decorations.

Effie held on to Manny and Manny held onto Tilly while she reached—quite dangerously—over the edge of the trampoline, gathering in all of the shoes. Then they flew back down to the castle, where everyone was waiting in the big hall, stamping their blue feet to try to keep them warm.

They all put their shoes on and their feet turned rosy pink and their clothes turned red and yellow and pink and green, orange and purple and blue … and even some tartan. And their hair turned black and brown and red and gold.

When Annabel put one shoe on, her grey dress and leggings turned the softest and brightest of green—the sort of green you find in the depth of the forest when the sun is shining and her hair turned slowly from silver to the deepest glossy **black**—just like Tilly's.

When she put the other shoe on, all the fireplaces magically filled with logs which burst into huge flames and heated the castle up in no time at all. Everybody had enormous smiles on their faces and their cheeks glowed with warmth—even Tabitha's. She was now dressed in beautiful **red velvet** with gold braid.

The cook turned on all the ovens and hobs and made the children delicious cheesy pasta which they ate at a huge table in front of a massive fire. When they'd finished, Tilly said sleepily, 'I think we should go now.'

'It's been lovely meeting you,' said Tabitha in her very posh voice. 'Thank you so much for all you have done for us and do visit us again very soon.'

'Oh yes, do!' said Annabel. And they all hugged and then climbed back on the trampoline again. Right away, the wind lifted them up in the air and soon all they could see of the castle was the warm glow from the windows.

'I really don't think I'll have another tantrum ever,' thought Tilly, as they sped off into the stars, 'but I *am* going to practise skipping.'

In the distance they could see their island. The sky became light again and the clouds turned pink with the rising sun.

'How long have we actually been away this time?' asked Effie.

'A whole day and a night,' replied Manny nervously.

'Remember,' said Tilly, 'clocks don't work. It's part of the magic.'

The other two still looked a bit worried. But they needn't have. When they went in the kitchen door, there was Shayjay coming down the stairs in her pyjamas.

'Been out already? Well, you must be hungry. I'll get some breakfast right away.'

The children looked at each other. They weren't hungry at all. They were full of cheesy pasta but of course they couldn't tell Shayjay that.

Acknowledgements

Many thanks to Arthur Cross, Bob Hay and Lorna MacKinnon who sowed the seeds of a great idea which Sarah Campbell and I immediately took up to produce this series of books.

The children of the island primary school 'road-tested' the stories and made valuable suggestions. Thanks, guys!

Thanks also to Adam Mahon, Ruben Campbell-Paine, Amy Bowman and Issy Budd who acted as models for some of the characters.

First published in softback in Great Britain in 2008 by Wigwam Press

Wigwam Press Ltd, 204 Latimer Road, London W10 6QY

Text copyright © Sarah Rowden 2008
Photography © Joanna Vestey 2008
Illustrations © Mark Beech 2008
Book design by Mary Till
Artworking by Brandammo Ltd
Assistant Photographer by Alex Sunshine
Production support by Resolution Creative Ltd

ISBN – 13: 978-0-9552192-2-1

A CIP catalogue record for this title is available from the British Library.

Printed in China.

This is the second book in a series – for more information or to order online please visit www.pollyandjago.com

Custard and Crayons

with

Polly & Jago